W9-BNR-167

THE SECRET OF SAGAWA LAKE

MARY LABATT

KIDS CAN PRESS

Kids Can Press acknowledges the financial support of the Ontario Arts Council, the Canada Council for the Arts and the Government of Canada, through the BPIDP, for our publishing activity.

Published in Canada by
Kids Can Press Ltd.
29 Birch Avenue
Toronto, ON M4V 1E2

Published in the U.S. by
Kids Can Press Ltd.
2250 Military Road
Tonawanda, NY 14150

Edited by Charis Wahl
Designed by Marie Bartholomew
Typeset by Rachel Di Salle

Printed and bound in Canada by Webcom

CM 01 0 9 8 7 6 5 4 3 2 1
CM PA 01 0 9 8 7 6 5 4 3 2 1

Canadian Cataloguing in Publication Data

Labatt, Mary, date.
  Secret of Sagawa Lake

(Sam, dog detective)
ISBN 1-55074-887-4 (bound)   ISBN 1-55074-889-0 (pbk.)

I. Title. II. Series: Labatt, Mary, date. Sam, dog detective.

PS8573.A135S42 2001   jC813'.54   C00-932857-2
PZ7.L32Se 2001

Kids Can Press is a Nelvana company

To my parents —
with my love

1. A Cottage up North

Sam stretched out in a pool of sunlight on the back porch and sighed. *Woodford is the most boring place in the world.*

Closing her eyes, she listened to voices from the kitchen. Joan and Bob were talking about working overtime.

Sam groaned. *Terrific. I'll be stuck in the house every day. Even weekends. If anybody cares.*

Just then a girl with long brown hair and a gentle face came out of the house next door. Ten-year-old Jennie Levinsky waved. "Hi, Sam!"

Joan and Bob had hired Jennie to take Sam for walks when they were at work. Now Jennie was Sam's best friend.

Sam sat up. The hair over her eyes moved up and down. *Bad news over here, Jennie.*

Sam and Jennie had a wonderful secret. All her life Sam had been trying to get humans to understand what she was thinking. When Sam met Jennie, she knew Jennie had the gift. *I can always tell when someone's got it,* Sam had told Jennie. *Most dogs are too stupid to notice.*

Jennie was thrilled. Sam's thoughts rang in her head like an echo. No one else could hear Sam, not even Jennie's best friend, Beth Morrison. And no one knew the secret except Jennie, Beth and Sam.

Jennie hopped over the fence and giggled when she saw Sam's angry look. "What's the matter, Sam?"

Sam flopped back down on the porch. *Joan and Bob don't deserve a beautiful dog like me. They're going to work overtime again. They don't care how bored I get.*

Sam looked up through the hair over her eyes. *And they're trying to make me eat dog food. I'm starving.*

Jennie fished in her pocket and pulled out two cream cookies. "I'm always prepared," she laughed.

Sam gobbled the cookies and licked her chops. *Let's go to your house. I need a good breakfast.*

Sam climbed up on Jennie's bed and put her head on the pillow. *I wish I could live with you. I hate my life.*

"You'd have to put up with a thirteen year old." Jennie's brown eyes twinkled. "Did you forget about my brother, Noel?"

Sam looked up. *Yuck. I don't want to live with a lout.*

"What's a lout?"

A lummox. A big oaf. A teenager.

Just then Jennie's mother poked her head in the door. "Jennie," she asked brightly, "did your dad tell you the good news?"

Jennie was puzzled. "What news?"

"We're going up to Sagawa Lake on the long weekend!"

"Sagawa Lake!" cried Jennie in dismay. "But it takes hours to get there!"

"That's why we like it," said Mrs. Levinsky. "No cars. No telephone. Nothing but wilderness."

Sam suddenly looked suspicious. *Wait a minute. Don't bears live in the wilderness?*

"There's nothing to do up there, Mom," whined Jennie.

"Noel's complaining, too." Jennie's mom shook her head. "I don't understand it. It's wonderful to see unspoiled country."

What's so wonderful about it?

"Can I take Sam and Beth?" Jennie begged. "There's nothing there! I need my friends!"

Yeah. Sam sat up, her pink tongue hanging out. *Take me. If you don't, Joan and Bob will shove dog food down my throat. That is, if they ever come home.*

But Jennie's mother was gone. Sam turned to her friend. *Wilderness, huh?*

"Yeah," said Jennie glumly. "And I hate wilderness."

Sam closed her eyes and pictured endless trees. *No ice-cream stands. No pizza. Bears making their messes everywhere. Wolves prowling around. Hmm ... Maybe I should stay home.*

"You can't stay home, Sam! I'd be bored without you!"

Bears are worse than dog food.

"Come with me." Jennie reached out and hugged Sam.

Well ...

"I'll bring tons of snacks."

Okay. That settles it.

Maybe I can stand it for one weekend.

It didn't take Jennie long to convince her parents to take Sam and Beth.

"Taking Sam will help Joan and Bob," said Mrs. Levinsky. "And Beth is always welcome."

Beth was thrilled. "I love the wilderness!" She clasped her hands. "We'll see what the world looked like before people wrecked it!"

Jennie and Sam exchanged looks. "Should I tell her how boring it's going to be?" whispered Jennie.

Sam shook her head. *No way. She might stay home.*

Beth didn't notice. "Hey! Maybe we'll see a beaver dam!"

Now there's a thrill.

"Or a moose!" Beth's fluffy red hair bounced and her bright green eyes sparkled.

More big messes on the ground. Sam shuddered. *How am I supposed to walk around in this place?*

Jennie giggled.

You can laugh. You've got shoes. I have to walk around on my bare paws.

Jennie threw back her long brown hair and laughed out loud. "Sam's worried about animal messes in the forest."

But Beth wasn't listening. "Just think, Jennie!

We're going to step in the footsteps of the pioneers!"

We're going to step in somebody's big mess, that's what we're going to step in.

"We'll see clean lakes filled with fish." Beth's eyes grew dreamy.

Who cares about fish? I need a mystery — not a fish.

Beth paced back and forth happily. "Maybe we'll see an animal that's almost extinct …"

Jennie and Sam looked at each other.

I thought you said wilderness was boring.

"I did."

Listen to our friend over there.

Jennie looked puzzled.

If you ask me, she gets the boring prize.

2. Driving to Sagawa Lake

When the day came to leave, Beth arrived lugging three huge books about wildlife. She put them on the back seat of the van.

Sam nudged Jennie. *Tell her not to read any of that junk out loud.*

"Shh," whispered Jennie. "If I said that, it would hurt Beth's feelings."

It'll hurt my feelings if I have to listen to her read.

Without a word, Noel and his friend Jason climbed into the middle seat. As usual, they had music blaring from their earphones. They looked around blankly.

No wonder teenagers are boring. Sam snorted. *Their brains have turned to mush from all that noise.*

Sam nestled cozily on the back seat between Jennie and Beth. *Where's the food? I'm hungry.*

"But we're still in the driveway."

So? Get out the cookies. And the jelly worms and the nacho chips and the cheese puffs. I need —

"Sam!" interrupted Jennie. "The drive takes hours! We can't eat everything now."

Hmph. Well … we don't want to starve.

The car droned on and on — past houses, through towns, past factories. The humming tires made Sam sleepy. She shifted uncomfortably. *I'm getting stiff and grumpy here — if anybody cares.*

Beth settled in the corner and read one of her books. Whenever she started to read something aloud, Sam glared at her. Most of the time Jennie slept.

After what seemed like a lifetime, Sam noticed forests gliding by the windows. She groaned. *I knew it. There's nothing up here but trees.*

Sam looked around the van. Jennie was snoring lightly. Beth was reading. Noel and Jason were still listening to music that blasted out of their earphones. In the front, Mr. and Mrs. Levinsky talked quietly. Past the windows glided a never-ending green blur.

"I'm sure the turn is coming up," Jennie's father said.

"It's been four years since we were here. I can't quite remember what the sign looks like," answered Jennie's mother.

She slowed down the car and peered at a weathered sign. "Look! Loomatchie. That's the old ferry landing, isn't it?"

Mr. Levinsky nodded. "That's our road." Carefully his wife turned the car into a rutted dirt track in the forest.

Hey! Wait a minute. This isn't a real road. We'll get lost in here!

Sam looked out the back window. The woods were dark and deep and silent. Tall pines soared upward. Overhead there was no sky – only branches.

Sam shivered. *Huge bears could be hiding in this forest.* The van rocked over the dirt track. *We're going to get stuck! There's nobody to rescue us!*

Jennie stirred. Beth closed her book. Even Noel and Jason looked up as the car hit the ruts.

At last the van lurched into a small clearing. A tumbledown shanty and a weathered gray dock stood on the edge of a lake. Dark water sparkled in the sunlight.

"We're here!" cried Mrs. Levinsky.

All around the lake crowded dense woods. Sam shuddered. *No houses. No people.* She shivered again.

The family stepped out of the van into a new kind of silence. Sam listened. There wasn't a sound from the shining water of Sagawa Lake.

Beth looked around excitedly. "Isn't it beautiful!" she whispered in awe.

Sam looked around at the vast silent emptiness.

Phooey.

I'll never find a good mystery in a bunch of trees.

3. A Strange Warning

THIS IS VERY INTERESTING...

A battered motorboat bobbed beside the dock. It was the only sign of life.

"Hello!" Jennie's father called. He turned to the shack. "Is anyone here?"

After he knocked, the door creaked open and an old man emerged. He looked like a hermit. His clothes were tattered and his white hair was wild.

"Hello yourself," he growled, spitting into the weeds by the door.

"It's Henry, isn't it?" asked Jennie's father politely.

"Henry's the name." The old man squinted at them. "Do I know you folks?"

"We haven't been here for four years," explained Jennie's mom. "We've rented the Anderson cabin on Winnewago Island."

Henry eyed them curiously. Then his gaze rested on Sam. "Mighty strange-looking animal you got there."

Sam bristled. *Mighty beautiful looking, you mean.*

Henry shook his grizzled head. "Never saw a critter like that before. Looks like a long-haired goat."

Noel and Jason guffawed.

Sam glared. *You don't look so good yourself, Henry. Tell him to shut up, Jennie.*

"I can't," whispered Jennie, leaning down to Sam. "It would be rude."

How come he gets to be rude and we don't?

Jennie covered Sam's ears. "Don't listen to him."

Phooey.

Mr. Levinsky smiled hopefully at Henry. "The Andersons said you'd have a boat ready for us."

Henry waved toward the battered aluminum motorboat. "There she is. Take it or leave it. But don't complain about it." Limping, he led them down to the rickety dock.

Jennie's parents followed meekly.

"The boat looks just fine," Mr. Levinsky said.

In horror, Sam looked down at the slime-covered boat bottom. *I'm not putting my feet in that yucky green gunk.*

Everyone went back to the van to get the bags and started loading the boat. When it was Sam's turn to get in, she jumped on a narrow seat and tried to keep her balance.

"We'll have to hold her, Beth," said Jennie, squeezing in beside Sam. "She doesn't want to step in that slimy stuff."

I wish somebody would make me some boots.

Henry helped them start the motor. After a few pulls, it sputtered to life.

As he was climbing out of the boat, Henry fixed the girls with an odd look. "You kids scared of this lake?"

We're never scared.

"Why should we be scared?" asked Beth.

Henry chewed his wad of tobacco slowly. "This is a mighty deep lake."

Sam watched the old man closely. *So, what's the big deal about deep?*

"Really?" Jennie tried to sound polite. She looked at Noel, but he and Jason were listening to music again.

Henry grinned, drawing his lips back from his brown teeth. "I bet you won't go swimming."

What's this guy trying to tell us?

Henry winked at the girls. "Sagawa Lake has a secret, you know."

The hair over Sam's eyes moved up and down. *Hmm ...*

Jennie and Beth began to feel nervous. "A secret?" asked Jennie.

Sam looked curiously at Henry's seamed face. *Secrets are good. As long as they're scary.*

Before Jennie could ask about the secret, her dad put the motor in gear. "Yes, well ...," he said, "I don't think we have to worry. The lake's too cold to swim, anyway."

Henry turned watery eyes on Jennie and Beth.

They gulped.

Henry spat into the weeds again and waggled his knobbly finger. "Be warned kids. Folks who don't listen are sorry."

"Oh, we'll be careful." Mrs. Levinsky smiled cheerfully.

Henry stroked his whiskery chin. "Being careful might not be enough."

Sam's head whipped up. *This sounds good!*

"We'd better be going," said Mr. Levinsky firmly. "Thanks for renting us the boat, Henry." He put the motor in gear and steered out across the sparkling waters of Sagawa Lake.

Henry waved to them from the dock. As they watched, he got smaller and smaller.

Sam nudged Jennie. *Find out about the secret.*

"Do you know the secret of the lake?" Jennie asked her parents.

Her dad shrugged. "Nope. I imagine it's some old campfire story that's been passed on over the years."

"I wonder what it is," mused Beth.

"Those stories are just for fun," said Mrs. Levinsky firmly.

"But Henry said if you don't listen you might be sorry!"

"Local people love to scare tourists like us," laughed Jennie's mother. "That's why we didn't let him tell the story. We won't have a good time if you kids get scared."

Mr. Levinsky looked back at the tiny figure against a sea of trees. "I think Henry's been alone too long. Don't worry about a thing he said."

Sam looked around the lake happily. *Who's worried? Secrets are great.*

The scarier the better.

4. A Lonely Island

Sam's mind whirred as the boat slid past pine-covered shores. *Deep lake ... a secret ... scared of the lake ... not swimming ... folks are sorry ... Hmmm ...*

Only the sputtering motor broke the silence of the lake.

"Smell this wonderful fresh air!" Jennie's mom took a deep breath.

Farther and farther into the lake they went, past rocky islands, through a narrow channel and then out into a wide glistening expanse of water.

Hmm ... This must be the deep part. Sam looked over the side of the boat at the black water. Instantly she pictured a scaly sea monster lurking in the depths. Its nostrils were flared and its back was studded with spines.

I bet there's an underground kingdom down there. All the creatures in the lake are under the sea monster's command. Sam closed her eyes and pictured mermaids swimming into the monster's castle.

She saw herself sitting on a golden throne beside the sea monster. He gave her an air hose to breathe with and told her she was the smartest dog he had ever met. Plates of lobster and shrimp were set before her.

All the lake people bowed. "Sam the wonder dog!" they cried. "She's the favorite of our king."

"Sam!" Jennie poked her in the ribs. "Stop daydreaming. We're almost there."

Sam looked up. A lone island rose out of the lake on a bed of rock. Jagged pines covered the land like a giant's beard.

Mrs. Levinsky sighed happily.

"We have three whole days to soak up all this peace and quiet!" exclaimed Mr. Levinsky.

Jennie leaned over and whispered in Sam's

ear. "See? There's nothing to do here and they love it."

But Sam was shaking hands with the lake monster and all the newspapers were taking pictures. She blinked at Jennie. *Huh?*

"Boring," repeated Jennie. "Look around, Sam. There's nothing here."

Beth was looking at the island with shining eyes. "It's wonderful, Jennie!"

Sam shot Beth a nasty look. *Don't start yakking about wilderness.*

The boat drew closer to the island.

It loomed before them — dark and lonely.

Long shadows snaked over the rocky shore. There was a sagging dock and an old aluminum rowboat tied to one of the posts. It was ghostly quiet.

Hmm ... Maybe I can find a mystery around here after all.

5. Clues for Sam

Everyone looked up at the dark island. Under gloomy pines squatted an old log cabin with a weathered wooden porch. Its windows stared back, blank and empty.

The silence was thick. Without a word, they climbed the rocky path to the cabin.

Inside, it looked like a trapper's cabin in an old movie. Snowshoes hung on log walls and a rusty woodstove surrounded by lumpy sofas stood in the middle of the room. Along one wall was an iron pump, a sink and a log table.

There's got to be a mystery in a place like this. Sam sniffed the musty air. *Maybe the ghost of an old trapper ... murdered by gold thieves ...*

Jennie, Beth and Sam had a small bedroom with rough wooden bunk beds.

"I love it here," breathed Beth, looking around with big eyes.

Don't start.

Beth unzipped her sleeping bag and spread it out on the top bunk. Jennie spread hers on the bottom. Suddenly they stopped –

A long, low moan came from the lake, mournful and sad.

Sam cocked her ears. *Aha! There's the ghost.*

"What's that?" asked Jennie.

Oooo. Ooooo. The sad sound rang across the lake.

It's the ghost of the old trapper. He –

"Don't start thinking about ghosts, Sam," interrupted Jennie.

Sounds like a ghost.

Beth raised her eyebrows. "Maybe it is a ghost."

Oooo. Ooooo. The call sounded so lonely it was heartbreaking.

Yeah. Some poor ghost girl is waiting for her true

love. She calls every day but he never comes ...

Jennie rolled her eyes. "Sam's talking about some dead girl calling to her lost love."

Beth's eyes took on a faraway look. "You never know with ghosts."

I love Beth.

Ooooo. Ooooo.

And I love ghosts.

"There's no such thing as ghosts," objected Jennie. But neither Beth nor Sam seemed to hear.

Beth sat down slowly on the edge of the bunk. "It must be a sad story."

Just then Mr. Levinsky popped his head in the door. "Hear the loons?" he asked.

The three friends looked up. "Loons?"

"Listen."

Ooooo ... Oooooo.

"Sounds sad, doesn't it?" And he was gone.

Sam shrugged. *Well ... it could have been a ghost.*

Jennie fixed Sam with a long look. "Don't you dare get us into trouble, Sam."

Sam gasped. *That's a very mean thing to say.*
I never got anybody into trouble in my life!

That night, Jennie and Beth snuggled into the musty bunks while a flickering lantern made shadows on the log walls. The loons were still calling on the lake.

Sam climbed onto the bottom bunk and settled down at Jennie's feet. *They're driving me crazy. Why don't they shut up?*

Jennie grinned. "Sam wants the loons to shut up."

"So do I." Beth wiggled deep into her sleeping bag.

For a few minutes they lay still in their beds, watching the lantern light waver on the wall. Everything felt strange and dark and sinister.

"What'll we do tomorrow?" Jennie asked at last.

Look for a mystery. What else would a great

detective like me do?

Beth's voice drifted out of the shadows. "I want to collect rocks. And I brought a book on northern trees, so —"

Tell her to shut up, Jennie.

In spite of herself, Jennie giggled.

Beth was puzzled. "What's so funny?"

"Sam wants you to shut up."

Beth laughed. "I bet she thinks that stuff is boring."

"She sure does."

Worse than boring. Let's talk about mysteries.

"We are not talking about mysteries, Sam." Jennie was firm. "There's nothing up here but woods, so how could there be a mystery?"

That old guy was hinting about something.

"He was teasing us because we're tourists."

No he wasn't. He was giving us clues.

"There are no clues!" Jennie sat up and bumped her head on the top bunk.

Beth leaned over the edge and looked down into Jennie's bunk. "Sam's talking about what Henry said, isn't she?"

"Yeah. She thinks he was giving us clues to a mystery," Jennie muttered.

"Maybe he was." Beth was thoughtful. "He doesn't think we'll swim ... and he made it sound like there's something to be afraid of ..."

Jennie rubbed her head.

"And the lake is deep ..." Beth went on slowly.

"So the lake is deep," scoffed Jennie. "That's nothing."

Beth was thinking. "But there's a secret here."

Beth's got the idea, Jennie. Those are clues!

"They are not clues!" exclaimed Jennie.

But Sam was humming happily to herself. *Look out, Sagawa Lake.*

There's a big secret here ...

And it's about to be uncovered by the world's greatest detective!

6. Sam Finds Something

The night was long and spooky. Through the darkness, the loons called to each other about the secret of the lake.

When the first shaft of sunlight shone through the window, Sam stood up on the bed. *Okay. Let's go!*

She nudged Jennie's feet with her round black nose. *I want buttered toast with ketchup. Pancakes with butterscotch sauce. And chocolate cake.*

She stepped on Jennie's lumpy form as she paced back and forth on the bunk. *Wake up. I'm bored.*

"Oof! Ouch!" came Jennie's muffled voice from inside the sleeping bag.

Jennie poked her head out sleepily. She looked at her watch. "It's only five o'clock!"

You don't want to sleep all day do you? There's a mystery out there. Let's get it solved.

"Go back to sleep!" hissed Jennie.

Hmph. No need to be grouchy.

"Stop stepping on me! You bad dog!"

Watch who you're calling bad. Sam hopped off the bunk. *I hate grumpy people.*

Rumpled and groggy, Beth peered over the top bunk. "What's going on?" she whispered.

"Sam wants to get up," Jennie whispered back, "and it's only five o'clock!"

"Forget it, Sam." Beth's head disappeared.

Humans are such creeps. No dog would yell at you for saying good morning.

Sam crawled underneath the bunk to sulk. *There'd better not be any spiders under here, or I'm going to bite somebody.* She put her chin on her paws. *I come to this stupid place where there's nothing but trees, and this is how they treat me.*

Sam wriggled back into the corner. *Ouch!* Something on the wall was poking into her back.

She shifted again. *There's something sticking out of this stupid wall.* She turned around to sniff at the logs.

Jutting out at an odd angle was a short log.

Sam sniffed around its edges. The log smelled of mold and old wood. Then she picked up a new smell. *So, what's this?*

Wafting through the musty logs was the faint, faint smell of leather. *Hmm ... This is interesting.*

Crawling on her belly, Sam sniffed up and down the log wall. She sniffed the bottom of Jennie's bunk and she sniffed the wood floor. *Aagh! Nothing but damp, dusty, old wood.*

Then she nosed back to the small log that stuck out. *There it is! Hmm ... Smells like shoes.*

For a few minutes, Sam lay under Jennie's bunk puzzling about the smell. *Maybe the leather smell is a money pouch. People always put money in special hiding places ...*

Hey! Maybe it's the old trapper's gold. It's in a leather sack. There's gold hidden in that wall!

Sam crawled out and pulled on Jennie's sleeping bag. *Get up! I found something!*

"Go away," groaned Jennie, clutching the sleeping bag around her.

But Sam pulled harder. *There's something in the wall. We're rich!*

Jennie groaned louder.

Beth's legs swung over the side of the bunk. "What's going on?"

"This crazy dog says she's found something," muttered Jennie.

Watch who you call crazy. Sam tugged at the sleeping bag again. *It's under the bunk. Something's hidden in the cabin wall!*

Jennie opened her eyes sleepily. "Something's hidden?"

Yeah. Like gold. Don't be so lazy. We're rich!

Beth jumped down from the top bunk. "What's Sam talking about?"

"She says she's found gold and we're rich." Jennie reached for the sleeping bag and pulled it over her again. "We can be rich later."

Beth grinned at Sam. "Show me, Sam."

Sam crawled under the bunk and wriggled over to the wall. Beth followed, squirming along on her stomach.

Sam sniffed at the edges of the log and whined. Beth picked at it. "It's loose!" she exclaimed. "I need a flashlight."

Beth wiggled out and rooted around her bunk for her flashlight. "Come on, Jennie. Sam's found a loose log in the wall! I think there's something hidden in there!"

Sighing, Jennie got up and grabbed her flashlight, too.

Together, the girls crawled under the bunk.

Over here, Jennie. Shine your light on this log.

Jennie shone her light. A small log stuck out at an odd angle as if it had been wedged there in a hurry.

Jennie and Beth grabbed at the edges of the log and jiggled it. The log moved!

"Slide it back and forth," whispered Beth, pulling as hard as she could.

Suddenly, the log slid out. Jennie and Beth shone their lights into a small space in the wall.

Nestled between the log beams was a stained brown leather book with a lock. An old-fashioned brass key lay beside it.

The girls gasped.

Sam chortled. *I knew it!*

Beth grabbed the book and Jennie grabbed the key. Propping themselves up on their elbows, they edged backward out from under the bunk.

Sam was right behind them. She shook herself and danced a happy little dance across the floor. Her head started to whir. *I love a mystery.*

I bet there's a treasure map! I bet there's a ghost! I'll be famous and I'll be on TV. Sam stopped dancing and stared suspiciously at her friends. *I'm going on the TV shows. Don't try to hog the fame just because I'm a dog.*

But her friends weren't listening. Holding their breath, Jennie and Beth were leaning over their prize.

And Beth was turning the key!

7. A Message from the Past

JUST GET THE CLUES.

The lock sprung wide and Beth opened the wavy brittle pages with a crackle. At the top of the first page was a faded date: June 5, 1937.

"1937!" exclaimed Beth. "That was ages ago!"

"Wow! Somebody's diary!" breathed Jennie, looking at the yellowed paper and watermarked leather. "This is really old."

Who cares how old it is. See if there's any clues.

Jennie read the first lines.

June 5, 1937. My name is Ruth. The cabin is finally finished and we've come to spend the summer on Sagawa Lake. I'm going to write in my new diary every day.

Okay, so she writes in this thing. Big deal. Skip the boring stuff.

Turning the brittle pages curiously, Jennie and Beth hunched over the old book. The handwriting was faded.

"She's ten years old!" cried Beth. "Like us!"

"Her family built this cabin!" added Jennie.

"1937 is the year they built it." Beth turned another page carefully.

That's back in the Stone Age. Find something interesting.

Jennie looked up from the spidery writing. "It's going to take a long time to read this, Sam. She wrote a lot."

Sam's face fell. *I hate reading. I refuse to sit around while you read.*

"But we need to find out what she said."

Sam stared. *I'm hungry.*

Jennie sighed. "Sam wants to eat."

Beth grabbed the diary and climbed back up to the top bunk. "This is fabulous. It'll tell us the history of this place."

Forget history. We need clues ... and food. First food.

Sam led Jennie out into the main room where she polished off chips, pop, cheese puffs with ketchup, and oatmeal cookies. Her belch echoed in the quiet cabin.

Sam grabbed a box of sugar-coated cereal with her teeth and headed back to the bedroom.

Let's see if Beth found anything interesting.

Beth was still on the top bunk, biting her fingernails and reading furiously.

"Well?" asked Jennie.

Beth jumped down. "I love this! Ruth would be an old lady now. It's like meeting someone from the past!"

Who cares? Did she say anything about a mystery?

"Sam wants to know if there's a mystery."

Beth shook her head. "I don't think so. She just talks about all the animals and how wild it is up here. She used to find gold nuggets in the water."

Gold! Sam sat up straight. *Gold is good.*

"Let's read some more," Jennie leaned over the diary eagerly.

As the girls read, Sam nuzzled into the sugar-coated cereal box and slurped happily. She pictured herself finding gold nuggets and being rich forever. Sam was thinking about the food she would buy when Beth interrupted.

"Look!" Beth cried, jabbing a finger at a faded page. "Ruth was scared of something!"

She read aloud:

> June 24, 1937. I am frightened of the secret of Sagawa Lake. My parents met an old prospector who believed it. That is why he painted the face on the rock. It is supposed to be a spirit to ward off the evil in the lake.

Evil in the lake? Yes! Sam dropped the cereal box. *Forget the gold. Rich is good, but a mystery is better!*

Beth looked up from the diary. "Ruth doesn't say any more, but she sounds really frightened."

"Evil in the lake," breathed Jennie. "That gives me a chill."

Hey! The old guy asked if we were scared, didn't he?

"Yeah."

Think about it. Being scared. Evil in the lake. Hmm ... Suddenly, Sam lifted her head proudly. *I know what the evil is.*

Jennie was puzzled. "Tell us."

It's a sea monster! Delighted, Sam whirled around. *Or maybe I should say a lake monster.*

"A monster!"

"Monster!" echoed Beth. She chewed on her lower lip. "Hey! Maybe it is ..."

It has a lovely sound, doesn't it? The monster of Sagawa Lake.

Sam hummed to herself. *This is great. Forget the reading.* She stared at Jennie. *I bet that monster's been here for a million years.*

"You m-mean like a dinosaur?"

Yup. Sam danced around the room in little circles. *Have you any idea how much a museum would pay for a real dinosaur?*

Sam stopped dancing. *Wait a minute.*
Hollywood would pay a lot more!

"We can't sell a dinosaur, Sam," objected
Jennie. "We couldn't even catch it."

Beth looked up from the diary. "What does
Sam want to do?"

Jennie rolled her eyes. "She wants to sell the
monster to Hollywood."

Beth grinned at Sam. "You're such a silly
dog."

Silly! Sam sniffed. *It's a brilliant idea.*

Beth grew thoughtful. "A lake monster ..."
She looked back at the diary. "Maybe Ruth says
more about it later."

She flipped carefully through the stiff pages.
"We've got another month and a half to read.
She doesn't stop until August twenty-third."

Enough reading. Sam marched to the door and
scratched.

I have to get a look at this thing.

8. The Face in the Forest

MAYBE WE CAME TOO FAR.

Stepping out into the early morning silence, the three friends noticed shafts of pale sun filtering through the trees. Only the small sounds of the forest broke the stillness.

Sam led them down the rocky path, the motorboat and aluminum rowboat bobbed next to the dock. Sagawa Lake sparkled in the sunlight, its secret buried deep beneath the surface.

Sam's mind was working furiously. *How do you find a lake monster when you can't swim?*

Jennie looked around. "I guess we could walk around the shore."

Yeah. We'll look for clues. Sam jerked her head toward the beach. *Come on. Let's explore.*

Jennie and Beth followed Sam. Along the edge of the beach crowded dense underbrush and deep forest. Sam kept looking up at the island in disgust. *I'm sick of trees.*

After they had walked for a while, the shore turned rocky. Sam sat down and snorted. *This is crazy. We won't find anything walking around this stupid island.* She looked down sadly at her paws. *And I hate having wet feet.*

That's it. Sam stood up and turned around. *We need a boat.*

When they got back to the cabin, everyone was up, and Mrs. Levinsky was cooking pancakes. "Pull up a chair," she said. "This fresh air will make you hungry."

Sam slipped under the log table and took her place beside Jennie's knee. *I want some dill pickles with these pancakes. Don't try giving me boring old butter.*

Over breakfast, everybody talked about the day's plans. Jennie's mom and dad said they wanted to relax and read. Noel and Jason wanted to get a tan and do some fishing.

When Jennie asked if she could use the rowboat, her mother and father were surprisingly agreeable.

"As long as it doesn't have any holes in it," said Mr. Levinsky. "I'll check it out."

"Let's check for spiders, too." Jennie shuddered. "I hate spiders."

"No problem," said Jennie's dad, smiling at the girls. "We'll take a broom and some spray. If there are any spiders, we'll get rid of them."

If I get spiders in my fur, there'll be trouble.

Mrs. Levinsky looked firmly at Jennie and Beth. "Remember, you have to wear life preservers."

"And you have to stay near the shore," warned Mr. Levinsky. He reached for another pancake. "We'll get the boat ready right after breakfast."

Spiders scuttled out of every corner of the rowboat and disappeared into cracks in the old dock.

"Yikes!" cried Jennie and Beth, screaming and jumping back.

Disgusted, Sam stayed on the shore and watched.

When all the spiders were gone, Mr. Levinsky hopped in the boat and inspected every corner. After awhile he straightened up. "Good news. The boat doesn't leak and there's not a spider left."

He gave Jennie a long look. "Promise me you'll stay close to shore."

Jennie promised.

Sam immediately forgot the spiders and hopped into the boat. Scrambling up to the bow seat, she sat proudly, her ears pricked up ready for adventure.

When Sam saw Jennie's father come toward her with a dog life preserver, she groaned. He put her legs through the holes and zipped it up.

I don't believe this.

"Sam can't go with you unless she wears this," said Jennie's dad firmly. "Sheepdogs aren't very good swimmers and their fur weighs them down. Sam would sink if she fell overboard."

I'm not going to fall overboard. Do I look stupid or something?

"Never mind if she doesn't like it," Mr. Levinsky continued. "Either she wears it or she stays with us."

Phooey. I should bite this guy.

Sam glared at Jennie's father as he climbed off the boat and undid the ropes.

"We'll make her keep it on," promised Jennie.

Sam glared at Jennie.

"We promise," echoed Beth.

Sam turned and glared at her.

Carefully, Jennie and Beth pulled on the oars. The boat started to move in a slow, lazy circle.

Hey! We want to go that way!

On the dock, Noel and Jason guffawed.

Sam shot them a nasty look. *I hope those spiders crawl up your pants.*

Jennie's mom yelled from the shore, "You have to pull together!"

After a few large circles, Jennie and Beth pulled the oars at the same time, and the boat moved forward.

Get some speed going here.

"Stay near the shore!" Mr. Levinsky called.

Jennie felt nervous and excited. "We'll be careful!"

Beth nodded, her eyes alight at the thought of exploring on their own.

Forgetting about the life preserver, Sam shivered as a delicious little tingle slithered up her spine. *Here we come, monster! Hey, Jennie! Got the camera?*

"I've got it, Sam," Jennie called back.

Sam hummed to herself as the little boat slipped through the water. *People who catch lake monsters are very famous. I'll be on the front page of the newspaper.*

The shore slid by. Sam looked at the never-ending forest in disgust. *This is ridiculous.*

Just when Sam began to think rowing along the shore was useless, the shoreline seemed to split. Jennie and Beth turned the boat and rowed toward the break in the trees.

"That's odd," said Jennie. "It looks as if we could go in there."

"Yeah." Beth craned her neck to see. "Maybe it's a river."

Sam's pulse raced. *Get closer! Hurry up!*

The girls rowed toward the opening. As they got closer, they could see a river. The banks of the river were sandy and the water was greenish. It looked like it flowed from deep within the island.

Let's go! Sam wiggled happily on her seat.

Very slowly, they turned the little boat into the river. Instantly the sunshine was gone. Like a dark canopy, trees arched over them.

Into the gloomy silence of the deserted island they went. Their skin crawled. "This is very s-s-spooky," Jennie whispered, looking into the shadows.

Sam chortled. *All the best things in life are spooky.*

Beth peered into the woods. Any kind of creature could be lurking in there.

Sam hummed a cheerful tune to herself.

Fearfully, Jennie looked at the trees on either side. "M-maybe there's wild animals in there."

Sam stopped humming instantly. *Like bears?*

"Yeah," muttered Jennie. "Like bears."

"Animals don't stay on islands," said Beth. "They run out of food and cross the ice to the mainland in winter."

Good. Sam shuddered. *I hate bears. I heard they eat dogs.*

Deeper and deeper into the forest they went.

All around them loomed the murky woods. Nothing moved. The only sound was the swish-swish of the oars.

The silence held them prisoner.

No one spoke.

Jennie shivered. She felt as if a hand could reach out of the trees and grab her.

At last they came to a bend in the river. The girls turned the boat. Darker shadows closed in on them.

Then Sam saw it.

Yikes! She toppled backward off the seat and scrambled to her feet, sliding on the boat's slimy floor.

"Eeeeeeeeeek!" Beth ducked.

Sam tried to wedge herself under a seat.

"Help!" Jennie covered her head with her arms.

High on a sheer rock leered a terrible, giant face!

9. The Monster's Lair

For a long moment the three friends couldn't move. Then Sam backed out from under the boat seat and squinted upward.

Staring back at her from high on the rock was an enormous face of pure horror. Its teeth were bared and its furious eyes blazed with hatred.

Looking closer, Sam saw that the face was painted on the rock.

Hey! She nudged Jennie, who was cowering behind her oar. *It's only a painting.*

Slowly Jennie lifted her head from her arms. "A painting?" she repeated blankly.

Beth opened her eyes. "A painting!"

Yeah. Somebody painted that big face on the rock.

Beth looked through her fingers at the huge face. Its sizzling anger bored into her. "It's horrible!"

"S-scary, isn't it?" Jennie's eyes were glued to the face.

It's only a painting! How bad can that be? Sam looked around calmly. *So ... what else can we find here?*

But Jennie and Beth were still staring at the face. "That must be the face Ruth talked about in her diary," said Beth slowly.

Jennie nodded. "What did she say about it?"

"Some old prospector painted it because of the secret."

"I remember. It's a spirit to ward off evil."

Sam stopped peering into the trees and looked at the face again. *Hmm ...* She looked at the dark river winding its way through the forest. *Maybe the monster lives up there.*

Jennie gasped. "What?"

That's it! I bet the monster lives farther up the river.

Jennie looked at the river as it disappeared

into the trees ahead. "Sam thinks the monster lives up there."

Beth gulped.

Sam scrambled up to the seat again. *Come on, Jennie. We need a picture of this guy.*

Jennie shook her head. "I don't want to go any farther, Sam."

Beth took a deep breath. "Let's just take a quick look."

Beth is such a nice kid. I'll take her on a talk show with me. Sam turned and fixed Jennie with a hard stare.

But I'm not taking any wimps.

On they rowed up the river, deeper and deeper into the forest.

At the front of the boat, Sam squirmed happily. *I love adventure.* She looked around with a chuckle. *This is the life.*

When they rounded a bend in the river, Sam

gasped. *Oho! Just like I thought!*

Gleefully, she turned around to the girls. *Isn't this fabulous?*

But Jennie and Beth were staring.

They were looking at the mouth of a cave!

10. Into the Cave

Jennie and Beth were too shocked to speak. From the far shore yawned an opening in the hillside. On both sides of the cave's mouth stretched a sandy beach.

Hurry up. Sam wiggled and squirmed. *I need to get in there.*

"Y-you don't w-want to go in, do you, Beth?" Jennie asked in a tiny voice.

Sam eyed Jennie suspiciously. *Don't get wimpy.*

"If there's a lake monster, I want to see it." Two red spots burned on Beth's cheeks. "Look in the box your dad gave us and see if there's a flashlight."

Come on, Jennie. This is terrific!

Jennie sighed and lifted the lid of the emergency box. Flares, extra ropes, a first-aid kit, matches and … two flashlights.

Sam jumped up and down on her seat. *Hurry up!*

The girls reached for the flashlights and flicked them on.

Sam turned back to the cave. *Stop wasting time. Good detectives get right in there and solve things.*

Very slowly Jennie steered the boat toward the mouth of the cave. "I'm not so sure this is a good idea," she muttered.

Stop fussing. It's a great idea.

Sam craned her neck to see what lay ahead. Jennie and Beth held their breath.

The tiny boat glided into the cave. Like an enormous shadow, the cave roof covered them in darkness. Jennie and Beth stopped rowing and shone their flashlights.

Before they could see anything, the cave suddenly came to life! Thousands of tiny squeaks filled the air!

"Bats!" cried Beth, covering her head.

"They get in your hair!" squealed Jennie.

Who cares? I'll bite the little creeps.

After a few minutes, the squeaks died down and Jennie and Beth shone the flashlights around again. In the flickering circles of light, rough rock walls appeared.

Beth raised her light higher. Long, spiky stone icicles hung from the roof of the cave. "Wow! This is beautiful," she whispered.

Give me a break.

"D-don't you think we should go back out?" Jennie's voice was tiny in the vast space.

No way! This is a great hideout for a monster. I bet it eats bats.

Jennie and Beth didn't speak. As they watched their lights waver over the stones, they saw that the cave was quite large. Dark water splashed against the sides.

Listen for the monster's breathing.

11. Footprints!

I LOVE THE WILDERNESS!

Their hearts pounded in their throats. Jennie's hands were sweating. Even Beth felt a little dizzy.

For a few heart-stopping minutes they steered the boat around the cave, shining their lights on the rocky walls and roof. As soon as the light left a spot, black shadows closed in again. Sam gazed hopefully into the darkness.

The girls felt as if the monster was going to jump out at them at any moment.

Relax. I have wonderful teeth.

"Forget your wonderful teeth, Sam," whispered Jennie, her voice echoing in the empty cave. "Monsters are bigger than bears."

Sam felt a quick stab of worry. *Bigger than bears!* Then she shrugged. *But it won't have big teeth like a bear.*

"Who says so?"

I say so.

Jennie sighed. "This dog is crazy, Beth. She'll get us all killed."

Beth's heart was pounding. Every shadow made her jump. "Maybe we'd better not stay too long."

Did I ever tell you I hate wimps?

The girls turned the boat around. "And I hate crazy dogs!" Jennie whispered. "What if that monster leaps out and drags us all to the bottom!"

I told you I have —

"I know!" hissed Jennie. "Wonderful teeth."

Quickly the girls rowed back toward the mouth of the cave. The monster was breathing down their backs! It was about to grab them!

Jennie and Beth leaned into the oars and rowed with all their strength. "Hurry!" grunted

Jennie. They pulled and pulled. The little boat shot forward.

Sam almost lost her balance. She tottered on the edge of the seat and glared. *Watch it.*

Out of the cave they rowed.

"Let's get to the lake," puffed Jennie.

Sam glared harder. *We're not going back yet. We have to explore the beach.*

Jennie didn't answer.

Sam gritted her teeth. *The beach, Jennie.*

"N-now she wants to check the beach, Beth." Jennie looked back at the cave and shuddered.

Beth's heart was slowing. Feeling safe out in the daylight, she smiled at Sam. "Good idea."

Jennie sighed. "Why do I have such weird friends?"

"Just one little look." Beth winked at Sam.

"Well … Okay, but I don't want to stay long."

Still eyeing the cave in case the monster jumped out, Jennie helped Beth row the boat to the far end of the empty beach.

Sam hopped out as soon as the boat scraped the sand. Sniffing, she dashed up and down the beach. *I can't smell anything suspicious.* Then she sat down and listened. *Hmm ... Not a sound.*

Both girls stayed in the boat. Jennie kept looking nervously at the woods.

Sam ran back to the boat. *Come on.*

"There's nothing here, Sam," said Beth.

Still Jennie didn't move. "L-let's go, Sam. I feel creepy here."

I'll tell you what's creepy. Wimps are creepy.

With a sigh, Sam hopped back in the boat. *Okay. We'll look at the other beach.*

Jennie frowned. "The other b-beach is no different."

Sam raised her tufty eyebrows. *Excuse me. I'm looking for clues here like a good detective.*

"W-what kind of c-clues are you looking for?" Jennie asked.

Beth pushed the boat off the sand and jumped in.

One of the monster's horns ... or one of his claws. Sam fixed Jennie with a long look. *Maybe even one of his victims.*

Jennie gasped. "Victims!"

Beth gulped. "Victims?"

The hair over Sam's eyes moved up and down calmly. *I'm going to be very famous.*

"How c-can you be f-famous when you're eaten up?" Jennie asked miserably.

Stop arguing. I need some clues for my case.

Slowly the girls turned the boat and steered past the mouth of the cave toward the other beach. "This is the last stop, Sam. And I mean it," said Jennie.

When the boat landed, Sam hopped out and nosed around the beach eagerly.

Half way down the beach she stopped in her tracks. *Yikes!*

She whirled around and looked back at the girls. *Here it is! Proof!*

This is the monster's cave!

"Sam's found something, Beth!" Jennie whispered.

The girls climbed out of the boat. The beach was hot and silent. Beth and Jennie eyed the forest nervously. Anything could be hiding in there.

Sam raised her chin proudly. *Over here! I told you I'd find a clue.*

Their hearts pounding, Jennie and Beth walked toward Sam.

In the sand they saw huge webbed footprints!

12. When the Monster Walks

LET'S MAKE A TRAP.

The webbed footprints went down the beach and disappeared into the underbrush. Sam started to follow. *I'll find him while he's sleeping.*

"No way, Sam." Jennie grabbed Sam's collar firmly. "My mom and dad will be getting worried. Besides, it's too dangerous."

Sam sat down with a thud. *They won't be mad when we get a million dollars for this thing! Buy them a new house.*

"We're not going in the woods!" Jennie hissed. "We have to get the boat back!"

"Yeah, Sam," added Beth. "If we stay out too long, Jennie's mom and dad won't let us have the boat again."

Sam considered this carefully.

Slowly she followed the girls back to the boat. *Okay, but we're coming back. That monster's in the woods and I want to get a look at him.*

Sam hopped haughtily into the bow. *I'm a wonderful detective.*

Sam was so busy thinking about how famous she'd be, she hardly noticed the boat ride home. She could see herself showing pictures of the footprints to the world's leading scientists. They took notes and talked about how clever Sam was. "The discovery of the century," they murmured as they scribbled in their notebooks.

Sam looked up with a start when the boat nudged the cabin dock. Noel and Jason looked up from suntanning, their earphones hanging stupidly from their ears.

Teenage oafs. Sam eyed them with disgust. *You miss everything.*

Back in their room, the girls pored over Ruth's diary, taking turns reading each page. Sam sat on the bottom bunk surrounded by corn chips and doughnuts. She sighed as she munched. *Why does everything involve reading?*

"Look!" Jennie cried. "Ruth says the prospector told them how to ward off evil!"

The monster you mean.

"Ruth doesn't call it a monster. She just says evil."

Sam shrugged. *Same thing.*

Jennie read a bit more. "She made masks like the one he painted on the rock."

Now, that's interesting.

Beth read the next page. "Ruth was scared all summer. Look what she says here."

Beth ran her finger under the faded ink:

July 11, 1937. Evil stalks Sagawa Lake at midnight. You must be indoors with the windows shut, lest it come in and grab you while you're sleeping.

Sleeping, huh? Sam looked at the window. *Does this thing want dogs?*

"It doesn't say anything about dogs." Jennie answered.

Suddenly she gasped. "Ruth says that evil walks on Winnewago Island under the full moon!"

What's a full moon?

"When the moon's round – like a big white plate." Jennie read to the end of the page.

"Did you look outside last night, Jennie?" Beth whispered, her face pale.

Jennie shook her head.

Beth's voice was hollow. "I can see outside from the top bunk."

Jennie and Sam glanced up at the little window beside Beth's bunk.

So?

Beth took a deep breath and looked hard at her friends.

"There was a full moon last night!"

13. What Should We Do?

STOP READING, I'M BORED!

Jennie gasped. "If there was a full moon, then the monster was walking around last night!"

Sam gobbled another doughnut. *Good. We'll set a trap and catch him.*

Jennie's hand flew to her mouth. "You can't trap a monster that big, Sam! It's left over from prehistoric times!"

"He'd swallow us in one bite and eat the trap!" cried Beth.

Sam suddenly remembered a movie where she saw a dinosaur eat a horse. The horse's kicking feet had stuck out of the dinosaur's enormous mouth. She shuddered as she remembered the crunch of the dinosaur's jaws.

Okay. Forget the trap. I'll think of something better.

Jennie and Beth decided to read the rest of the diary to see what else Ruth said.

As the afternoon wore on, Sam got bored. She polished off the doughnuts and asked Jennie for sardines. *I love sardines with raspberry sauce.*

"Don't have any raspberry sauce," said Jennie, without looking up. "And we don't have any sardines."

Phooey. All this reading is making me crabby.

Sam glared at the diary. *Just what's so interesting in there, anyway?*

"It's so weird." Jennie still didn't look up. "I feel like I know this girl!" She turned the page. "She made a mask like the one on the rock and stuck it to her window."

Beth chewed on a fingernail. "We should do that, too. Ruth says it will keep the monster away!"

Big deal ...What about food?

Jennie didn't answer. The girls read and read, Jennie twisting her long brown hair and Beth chewing her fingernails.

That's it! In disgust, Sam went out to the kitchen to look around. *Good. The food's in boxes where I can get at it.*

She poked her nose in all the cartons and came up with butterscotch cookies, nachos, marshmallows and cheese puffs. *Too bad I can't open the ketchup. But at least I won't starve.*

She dragged all the bags to the bottom bunk and started to rip them open. Jennie and Beth didn't look down from the top bunk.

They read all afternoon – pointing and exclaiming and re-reading bits until Sam thought she would die of boredom. *I hate reading! There should be a law against it.*

Jennie didn't answer, so Sam amused herself by finishing off all the snacks. Then she belched hugely.

Nobody even noticed. Sam was licking up all the crumbs when a sick feeling started in the pit of her stomach. Then her stomach slammed into her throat. She groaned. "Aa-a-a-a-gh."

Jennie and Beth leaned down and looked into the bottom bunk. Sam was lying on her side, panting.

"Are you okay, Sam?" asked Jennie.

I'm dying. Sam groaned louder. "Aaa-a-a-gh." *Your parents brought rotten food. They've poisoned me.*

Jennie looked in horror at the bags strewn all over the bunk. "You didn't eat all that, did you?"

Sam opened one eye. *Of course I did. And now I've got food poisoning. You should complain to your parents.*

"Sam!" screeched Jennie. "This is enough food for six people!"

"No wonder she looks sick," muttered Beth, jumping down.

Sam's stomach heaved dangerously. *Don't yell at me. I'll throw up on your bed.* She burped horribly. "Aa-a-a-a-gh."

Beth looked at Sam in amazement. "I can't believe you ate that much, Sam! You're a very bad dog!"

Sam lay back on the pillow and groaned. *I've got food poisoning and you tell me I'm bad.* She closed her eyes in misery. *I can't believe my friends insult me when I'm sick.*

You'll be sorry when I'm dead.

14. Noises at Night

That evening Mr. and Mrs. Levinsky lit a campfire. They looked and looked for the marshmallows but finally gave up.

"I guess we forgot them," sighed Jennie's mom.

In front of the cabin the family sat in a small circle of firelight. All around them the woods loomed dark and forbidding.

"A full moon." Jennie shuddered and looked up at the night sky.

Beth eyed the silvery moonlight sparkling on the water. "That's when the monster walks on Winnewago Island."

Sam lay quietly at Jennie's feet. For the first

time in her life she didn't want to eat anything.

She turned her head away when Jennie tried to give her a hot dog. *I'm taking a break from food. I'm on a diet.*

"No wonder she won't eat," Beth giggled. "There are four huge, empty bags in there!"

Sam shot her a terrible look.

"Joan and Bob are right, Sam," whispered Jennie. "You should eat dog food."

Here we are on a deserted island with a million-year-old lake monster, and you start the speech about dog food. Sam sniffed haughtily. *Don't talk to me until you have something interesting to say.*

"Get ready, everybody," cried Jennie's dad suddenly. "I'm going to tell a ghost story."

Sam's ears pricked up. *I love ghosts.*

Mr. Levinsky rubbed his hands together and started telling a story about a haunted castle. Two boys were trying to prove how brave they were by sleeping in the castle. At the stroke of midnight they heard a sound.

Jennie and Beth huddled together. As her father spoke, Jennie felt the darkness of the forest pressing in on her.

Relax, Jennie. He's telling a great story here. The bit about the ghost coming to the castle door with her head under her arm is great!

Jennie shivered. "I feel like the monster's going to reach out of the trees and grab me."

Beth gulped. "Me, too."

Noel and Jason lolled on the ground. "Make the story scarier, Dad!" shouted Noel. "How about some blood spurting out of the ghost's neck?"

Sam sniffed. *Trust a teenager to wreck a good ghost story.*

Jennie was getting more and more nervous. "I don't want to be out here at midnight."

Beth leaned into the firelight and looked at her watch. "It's eleven thirty."

Sam chortled. *Good. We should hear the monster any minute now.*

Jennie prodded Sam with her foot. "Maybe it will eat us!"

Oh ... The picture of the dinosaur chomping on the horse popped back into

Sam's mind. *Well ... we don't want that.*

The ghost story got so scary that Jennie and Beth plugged their ears.

"I'm tired!" shouted Jennie, just as the ghost threw her head at the owner of the castle.

"I hate little kids," moaned Noel. "The story was just getting scary!"

You want scary? Just keep your eye on those trees, Lummox.

"I'm sleepy!" screamed Beth in a panic. She looked at her watch. It was ten minutes to twelve.

Jennie's dad was surprised. "How can you be tired in the middle of one of my famous stories?"

"I guess they've had a big day," said her mom, shining the flashlight toward the cabin. "Come on, I'll tuck you in your bunks. Your dad can finish the story tomorrow."

"Finish it now, Dad," begged Noel. "Forget the little kids. And forget Samantha, the walking mop."

Sam stepped on his foot as she walked past.

At that moment, everyone froze.

"What's that?" whispered Jennie's mom.

Something was moving in the forest!

"I thought we were alone on this island." Mr. Levinsky sounded puzzled.

Crack! A twig snapped in the woods.

Everyone held their breath.

Leaves moved in the underbrush.

"We'd better go inside," he said.

"I don't understand this," Mrs. Levinsky muttered. "There's nobody else on the island."

Jennie and Beth started to run for the porch.

Crack! The thing was coming closer!

"L-let's g-go in!" screamed Jennie.

"Maybe it's a bear!" whispered Jennie's mom. "Mrs. Anderson said they had a bear once!"

"Everybody inside!" Jennie's dad sprinted up the stairs and they all piled in the cabin door.

When the door was firmly locked, Jennie grabbed her mother's arm. Her words tumbled out. "It's a monster, Mom! We found an old diary from 1937. It belonged to a girl named

Ruth! Her family built this cabin and she says there's a monster in this lake!"

"Yeah. And he walks on Winnewago Island at midnight!" panted Beth.

"Under the full moon!" added Jennie.

To her horror, Jennie's parents started to laugh.

"Now that would make a good story!" chuckled her dad. "I'll work on that one. Maybe my ghost stories are getting a bit old."

"Children had big imaginations back then, just like they do today," Jennie's mom smiled. "Now – bedtime."

Noel and Jason threw themselves on the sofa laughing. "Little kids are so stupid!"

Jennie's parents eyed the boys coldly and sent them to bed, too. "The bear will be gone by morning," Mr. Levinsky promised.

With a sigh, Jennie, Beth and Sam went into their room and closed the door. Beth looked at her watch. "It's midnight!"

Jennie was trembling. "G-good thing w-we put the mask in the window."

Sam looked up. *What mask?*

"We made a mask just like the one on the rock. Ruth said it would keep the monster away."

I don't remember making a mask.

Jennie hugged Sam. "You were too busy feeling sick."

Pulling the sleeping bags over their heads, the three friends cowered in the bottom bunk.

Then they heard it.

From outside came small sounds. The swish of water ... a clunk ... footsteps ...

Their hearts pounded and their palms started to sweat.

They waited ...

But the sounds didn't come any closer.

"The mask is working," whispered Beth.

At last the sounds went away, and they slept fitfully.

The night seemed to last forever.

15. The Next Clue on the Beach

YIKES! HE WAS HERE!

In the morning, Jennie, Beth and Sam stepped outside fearfully. Shafts of pale light shone through the tall trees. The only sound was the mournful cry of the loons.

Sam hopped off the porch and nosed around the pine needles. *The monster must have left a clue.* She sneezed. *I hate pine needles. They stink and they get up my nose.*

Jennie and Beth sat nervously on the porch steps.

Sam looked up. *You two are sure chicken this morning.*

Jennie nodded meekly. "We're not chicken. There's a monster here. Remember?"

Beth looked at Sam firmly. "Yeah."

There's nothing to worry about. Sam sniffed some underbrush. *The monster's not here.*

Jennie looked surprised. "How do you know?"

The diary said he walks at midnight, doesn't it?

Jennie poked Beth with her elbow. "Sam's right. The monster can't be here. It's daytime!"

A slow smile spread across Beth's face. "Why didn't we think of that?"

Because I'm the smart one. You two are just my assistants.

Beth hopped off the porch steps. "Good. Then it's safe to look around."

Sam headed toward the beach, sniffing and nosing her way to the path. *I don't see any footsteps ... or chewed up animals ... or any clues that a monster's been here.*

Jennie and Beth searched the ground.

"We should see some broken trees or something," said Beth. "Prehistoric monsters are huge."

Jennie looked at the underbrush. "It doesn't seem like anything big crashed through here."

Sam started down the path to the shore. *Let's look on the beach.*

Sam hopped onto the old wooden dock and looked out at the lake. Then she looked down at the sand.

Aha!

"What is it, Sam?" called Jennie, scrambling down the path. "What do you see?"

Beth slid down the rocks behind her. "What is it?"

Sam's eyes were glued to something on the beach. *Look! He was here all right!*

There, on their own beach were big webbed footprints! Just like the ones near the cave.

Jennie, Beth and Sam stared at the footprints going in and out of the water.

It's a lake monster for sure. Look. He always goes back underwater.

Beth and Jennie sat down on a log.

"What do we do now?" Jennie frowned.

"I'll get some paper to make a list of the clues," suggested Beth.

Sam whirled on Jennie. *Tell this kid not to write. If she starts writing it'll make me crazy!*

Jennie giggled. "Sam hates writing. Remember?"

Beth grinned. "Sorry, Sam. But I like to make lists so I don't forget things."

Sam sniffed. *Well ... make them when I'm not around.* She looked at Jennie. *Get the boat, Jennie.*

Time to go back to the cave.

Jennie went back up to the cabin and asked her parents if they could use the rowboat again. "No problem," agreed her father. "You did well yesterday."

"But stay near the shore," warned Jennie's mom. "And you all have to wear life preservers – even Sam."

"Don't run into any lake monsters," guffawed Noel, shoveling cereal into his mouth.

"Stop teasing your sister," said Mrs. Levinsky sternly.

Noel snickered. "Sorry."

When Jennie got back to the beach, Sam and Beth were already in the rowboat with their life preservers on.

"You should hear Noel and Jason laughing about the lake monster," Jennie muttered as she got in.

They untied the ropes and rowed out into the still lake. The sun was climbing in the sky and the day was getting warmer. Pine-covered shores slid past as they rowed.

Nobody spoke until they got to the break in the trees. As soon as they saw it, Jennie and Beth turned the boat into the river mouth.

The river met them in silence. Overhead, branches blocked the sun. Into the gloom they rowed.

"Y-you're sure the monster's n-not around?" Jennie asked nervously.

Quit worrying. We're safe until midnight.

Beth chewed her lip thoughtfully. "Ruth would have said if it walked around during the day."

Jennie gulped. "I guess s-so." Leafy underbrush crowded them on both sides.

The face on the rock suddenly shot out at them, leering horribly.

Jennie covered her eyes. "I can't get used to that thing!"

"Me either." Beth's cheeks flamed pink.

The river was getting narrower. Jennie gripped her oar with sweaty hands and swallowed hard.

"Spooky, isn't it?" muttered Beth.

Jennie didn't answer. They waited.

Rounding the bend in the river, the cave loomed before them on the far bank.

They were there.

Jennie and Beth steered the boat to the beach. With a scrape, the boat rubbed on the sand and stopped. The silence of the forest reached out for them.

Sam jumped off the boat with a thud. *Bring the camera, Jennie. We need a picture for the newspaper.*

Nosing around the beach, Sam dreamed about fame. *Newspaper headlines ... Hollywood ... talk shows ... movie contracts ...*

Suddenly she stopped in her tracks. *Well. Well.* She turned to the girls. *I knew it!*

Fearfully, Jennie and Beth climbed out of the boat and walked over to Sam. Then they looked at the beach.

More webbed footprints!

The hair over Sam's eyes rose and fell calmly. *See how it is? First he comes to spy on us and then he swims home.*

Get the camera ready.

16. Inside the Cave

YOU WON'T BELIEVE THIS!

Sam trotted toward the cave, humming happily to herself. *He's in there.*

Jennie didn't move. "I'm going back to the boat."

Beth nodded. "Me, too."

Sam shrugged and followed them. *Okay. The boat's good.*

They climbed in and pushed the boat away from the shore.

Beth looked at the mouth of the cave doubtfully. "Jennie, I really want to get a picture."

Jennie didn't move.

Come on. I'm getting old here. Let's go!

Jennie twirled her hair nervously.

Hey! I can't be a world-famous detective if you're too chicken to take a crummy picture.

"All right. I'm ready," Beth said suddenly, through clenched teeth. "Let's get that picture."

Jennie fidgeted. "I hope it's safe to go in."

Safe is boring. Think of the TV interviews. Think of Hollywood. Sam stared hard.

Jennie gripped her oar. "All right," she said at last. "But we're turning around the minute it gets too scary."

As the boat glided inside the cave, the three friends held their breath. Swish. Swish. Into the blackness.

Swoosh! Screech! Screaming bats whirled around them like a dust storm. Jennie, Beth and Sam didn't move until the squeaking stopped.

They listened. Nothing.

Shine the flashlights! Sam climbed up on the

bow of the boat.

Jennie clicked on her flashlight and a comforting light suddenly shone ahead of them.

Beth did the same.

They held their breath as the circles of light wobbled over the walls of the cave. Nothing but rock. They were alone.

Maybe he sleeps on the bottom. Sam looked down into the water.

She reeled back in shock! She almost lost her balance and toppled out of the boat. *Whoa! Something's going on down there!*

"Beth!" whispered Jennie. "Sam says something's happening in the water."

Wow! This is great!

Beth and Jennie peered over the side of the boat.

Jennie gave a little shriek.

Beth gasped. It couldn't be true.

But it was.

Under the boat, something was glowing!

17. A Good Look at the Monster

THIS GUY IS HIDEOUS!

"Turn off the flashlight!" hissed Beth. "We don't want him to see us!"

Immediately they plunged into darkness.

The three friends leaned over the side of the boat. The glow moved! It spun around in a lazy circle.

Jennie's fingertips tingled. Her head whirled as if she was going to faint.

Sam chortled gleefully as the light split and swirled through the water. *We've found his underwater city! Maybe those are water cars.*

Jennie wanted to turn the boat around but

she couldn't. Her arms and legs were frozen.

Gripping the side of the boat with white fingers, Beth just stared.

The eerie streaks moved gracefully under the water. Around and around — as if they were dancing to music only they could hear.

Beth leaned back from the edge of the boat. What if the monster reared up out of the water and swallowed them?

Sam hummed happily to herself. *Hey, Jennie. Stick the camera under the water and take a few pictures.*

Jennie couldn't answer.

Sam sighed. *A great detective needs assistants who don't wimp out.* Sam looked back down at the black water. Now the glow was moving to the back of the cave.

Look!

But Jennie was shaking. "W-we have to g-get out of here," she finally stammered.

With graceful movements, the underwater lights turned over and over toward the end wall of the cave. It was like a ballet.

"What's happening?" whispered Beth.

The only answer she got was the sound of Jennie's chattering teeth.

Sam was disgusted. *Wake up! Get the camera ready. I think the monster's coming up!*

Nobody moved. Their eyes were riveted to the glow as it traveled to the back of the cave.

Sam jumped up and down. *Get the camera!*

Still Jennie couldn't move.

Suddenly a shiny black blob broke the still surface of the water! Then another black blob appeared, outlined in the eerie glow from the underwater light.

Hey! There's more than one! Get a picture!

Beth and Jennie were frozen, their eyes wide.

One of the black blobs began to ooze up out of the glowing water. A dim shadowy shape rose before them. Jennie, Beth and Sam could see its outline against the underwater lights. A huge shadow was thrown against the back wall of the cave.

It was a monster!

They nearly fell out of the boat!

This guy is hideous!

The silhouette of the monster was more horrible than anything they had imagined. It looked like a giant frog with a huge humped back. Its long frog tongue was wrapped around its head.

That long tongue could suck up anything!

Even a dog.

18. It's Following Us!

SHOULD I TELL THEM?

Suddenly Jennie and Beth moved.

Grabbing at the oars frantically, they turned the boat around. As fast as they could, they rowed out into the bright sunlight.

Jaws clenched, gripping the oars with all their strength, they sped down the river.

Sam picked herself up from the bottom of the boat. *Oof! I think I broke a couple of ribs.*

Looking behind them anxiously, Jennie and Beth rowed furiously.

You should have told me you were turning.

Puffing and panting, Jennie and Beth finally slowed down.

At last Sam was able to climb back on the

seat. *That monster is sure ugly! Did you see its tongue? One slurp and you're dinner.*

"It looked like a huge frog," said Jennie, her heart thudding in her chest.

"There's two of them!" cried Beth.

"Do you think they're both the same? The other blob didn't come up to the surface." Jennie's voice shook.

"The diary didn't say one monster! It just said evil in the lake!"

I bet there's an army of them — frog blobs who suck up people. Sam thought for moment. *And they'd suck up a dog if they got one.*

Suddenly the shadowy forest was gone and they were out in the bright sunlight of the lake. No one would guess there were hideous creatures hiding in its sparkling depths.

I know what they are! They're dinosaur frogs.

"Dinosaur frogs!" repeated Jennie.

Beth blinked. "That's what they looked like. Like frogs left over from prehistoric times."

Jennie shuddered. "I don't want to be slurped up."

Relax. The monsters are back there in the cave and we're out here in the bright sunlight rowing down a lovely lake ... enjoying a nice warm day ...

Sam happened to glance down at the water. *Uh-oh!*

"What is it, Sam?" Jennie was alarmed.

Maybe I spoke too soon.

"Sam!" Jennie cried.

Beth looked worried. "Does Sam see something?"

Sam was peering over the side of the boat. *Hmmm ... Do you think these things tip over boats?*

"What things?" yelled Jennie. "What are you looking at?"

Sam kept gazing over the side.

"She does see something!" screamed Beth.

"I know she does! And she won't tell me what it is!"

Don't panic.

"Who's panicking!" screeched Jennie. "What are you looking at?"

Ugh ... Well ... if you really want to know ... something's following the boat.

"Something's following the boat!" Jennie shrieked.

"Following the boat!" yelled Beth. "Where?"

See for yourself, Jennie. It's on your side now.

Jennie looked over the side of the boat and screamed.

A long dark shadow slithered through the water beside them.

19. We Need a Picture

The shadow followed them until they got to the dock. Then it slithered off into the depths of the lake.

In a blur they tied up the boat, scrambled along the path and ran for their room. They slammed the door.

"The mask will keep him away!" panted Beth.

Sam hopped up on the bottom bunk and hummed to herself. *I wonder what these frog blob things like to eat.*

Jennie and Beth dove into the corner of the bunk and waited until their hearts stopped pounding.

"That thing followed us!" cried Beth, burrowing deep into the pillows.

It sure was ugly.

"Did you see its huge tongue and humpy back?" Jennie's brown eyes were wide.

"Yeah." Beth chewed a fingernail. "And there were two of them!"

Oh, there's loads of them ... Hundreds ... Maybe thousands. The lake must be full of them.

"Sam thinks the lake is full of those things!" Jennie shuddered.

Sam panted happily. *That's what the evil in the lake is. Sagawa Lake is full of dinosaur frogs!*

"I'm glad we're going home tomorrow," said Beth. "All we have to do is make it through the night."

Sam sat up. *Hey! Nobody took a picture! How can I be famous when I don't have anything to show the newspapers?*

"I'm not going near those things to take a picture, Sam," retorted Jennie. "You can be famous for another case. Something safer."

Sam glared.

Beth was thinking. "Sam has a point. If we've only got one night, we should get some proof."

"What?" Jennie blinked.

"This is an important discovery, Jennie." Beth's eyes grew dreamy. "Weird creatures left over from a million years ago. It's fabulous!"

Exactly.

"What's so fabulous about it?" muttered Jennie. "I think being home would be really fabulous."

But Beth wasn't listening. "We need a picture, Jennie. Sam's right. We're going to be famous."

You bet.

"I'm taking that picture — tonight." Beth clenched her fists.

Jennie looked at her as if she'd lost her mind.

Sam chortled happily. *Beth is such a nice kid.* She squinted at Jennie. *Not like some people I could mention.*

Beth set her jaw firmly. "That's what I'm going to do. I'll take that picture when the monster comes to our beach."

The day dragged on forever. Jennie's dad showed them how to carve wood. Her mom showed them how to dry wildflowers.

"How about a hike in the woods?" asked Mr. Levinsky.

Jennie shuddered. "I hate the woods."

Her parents looked at her oddly. "You don't have a very good attitude today," said her mother.

She has a great attitude. Trust me.

In the end, Jennie's parents went on a hike together. Jason and Noel fished from the dock.

Sam eyed the boys from the top of the hill. *Do you think we should warn them that they could get slurped right off that dock?*

Jennie shook her head. "Noel would laugh his head off if I tried to tell him."

Sam shrugged. *The world won't miss a couple of teenagers anyway.*

Night came and everyone gathered by the campfire. Mr. Levinsky told a new ghost story, but the girls didn't listen. Their ears strained toward the forest for every sound.

"We've had a wonderful time." Jennie's mom smiled in the flickering firelight. "I don't want to go home."

Jennie's dad grinned at Jennie and Beth. "I think the girls miss TV!"

Jennie and Beth tried to smile.

Beth looked at her watch. It was ten thirty. "Time for bed!" she shouted.

Mr. Levinsky raised his eyebrows.

"The fresh air seems to make everybody tired," Jennie's mother said in a surprised voice.

They put out the fire and headed toward the cabin.

Night settled over the island.

20. Spying at Midnight

An hour later, the cabin was quiet and everyone was asleep.

Everyone except Jennie, Beth and Sam. They crouched in the bottom bunk … waiting.

Beth shone the flashlight on her watch. "It's almost midnight." She grabbed the camera. "Let's go, Sam."

Sam hopped off the bunk. *Time for some great detective work.*

Heaving a sigh, Jennie followed Sam and Beth. "I can't stay here alone," she muttered.

Like silent shadows, the three friends crept through the sleeping cabin.

Jennie kept close to Sam.

Sam looked up at Jennie. *I don't know why you're so worried. All we need is a picture.*

Jennie just shivered.

Beth pulled the door open quietly and they slipped out into the night. Standing on the porch, they looked at the lake shining silver in the moonlight. All around them the forest crouched in darkness.

Without a word, they tiptoed toward the beach.

"Get behind those trees," whispered Beth, pointing to a clump of trees growing on the hillside. "We can watch the beach from there."

Sam sniffed. *Who made her the boss?*

Silently they crept down to the trees and crouched in the shadows. Beth looked through the camera lens.

Under a round white moon the still lake glistened and glittered.

They waited.

The lonely sound of the loons echoed through the night.

Still they waited.

Clouds drifted across the moon and the night turned pitch black.

They didn't move.

Sam suddenly gasped. She nudged Jennie with her round black nose. *Look!*

When Jennie peeked around the trees, she thought her heart would stop. She grabbed Beth's sleeve.

Coming across the lake, under the black water, was an eerie glow just like the one in the cave.

Slowly and silently, it moved toward them.

Jennie, Beth and Sam froze.

It was coming right at them!

Closer …

The glow flowed through the water.

Closer …

The three friends held their breath.

Then it was at the shore.

One shiny black blob popped up on the lighted water. Then another.

As they watched, the two blobs oozed toward the shore. Then the glow went out and the night was pitch black again.

In the darkness, Jennie, Beth and Sam listened. They could hear the swishing of water but they couldn't see anything.

Then a tiny shaft of moonlight peeked through a wispy cloud – for just a moment.

Jennie and Beth clutched each other and gasped. In that brief instant they saw a terrible shadow. They could make out two hideous creatures in the water. They had long tongues wrapped around their heads.

It was two frog monsters!

In the darkness, Beth stepped out from behind the trees. Creeping down the bank, she held the camera up to her eye. She couldn't see anything.

Silently Beth sneaked a little closer …

"Aaaa-a-a-a-a-h!"

Her foot got caught in a vine and she lost her

balance! The camera flew out of her hands. Grabbing wildly for something to hold onto, Beth tumbled over and over.

Behind the trees, Jennie clutched Sam.

Beth crashed down the hill ...

Right into the water!

21. Sam Finds out the Truth

Those monsters will drag Beth back to the underwater city!

"Grr-r-r-r-r," growled Sam.

She leaped out into the darkness. *I'll save you, Beth!*

Sam crashed down the black hillside. *You're not taking my friend, you frog-blob weirdos!*

"Woof! Woof! Grrr-r-r!"

Sam skidded down the hill and threw herself at the monsters who were standing up in the lake.

"Grrr-r-r. Woof! Woof!"

The monsters thrashed about in the shallow water.

"Oof!"

Sam jumped up and down, splashing and growling.

"Grrr-r! Woof! Woof! Woof!"

She glanced sideways and dimly saw Jennie helping Beth up.

Run! I can't hold these guys off much longer!

"Grrr-r! Woof!"

Beth and Jennie were staggering up the hill when lights popped up ahead of them.

Sam saw the lights. *Yikes! More monsters!*

"Grrrr!"

Sam crashed wildly around in the shallow water, barking crazily.

The lights were bobbing down the hill! *Watch out you frog things! There's a very tough dog here!*

Yelling sounded from all sides.

"Woof! Woof!"

The lights blinded Sam. Loud shouts rang in her ears.

Run, Jennie! I'll hold them off!

A sudden yank on Sam's collar stopped her. *Uh-oh. They got me!*

"Sam!" hollered a voice. It sounded just like Jennie's father.

Oho! So these monsters can imitate voices ... Very clever.

"Grrr-r!"

Then Sam looked up.

Mr. and Mrs. Levinsky and Noel and Jason were all around her. Everyone was yelling and waving flashlights. Mr. Levinsky was holding her collar.

Sam jerked backward and tried to pull out of the collar. *Let me go! There are a couple of lake monsters here!*

Then she looked beside her.

Two people were wading to shore. They wore black diving suits with air tanks on their backs. Hoses dangled from the air tanks.

Sam looked to her other side. Then she looked at the divers again.

So ... where did the monsters go?

Back in the cabin Jennie's parents made hot chocolate for everyone.

The two divers were named Bill and Marion. They glared at Sam over the rims of their mugs.

"That dog is crazy," muttered Bill.

"Absolutely nuts," agreed Marion.

Sam edged closer to Jennie's knee. *No need to be insulting.*

"If that dog had bitten me," growled Bill, "I'd have smacked it."

Sam squirmed. *No need to get violent.*

"Any dog that would bark at a couple of divers is stupid as well as crazy." Marion's eyes were angry slits.

Time to move on to another subject. Like lake monsters.

Mr. Levinsky apologized to Bill and Marion. "We are very sorry," he said. "We need to find out why the girls took Sam outside."

Instantly Bill and Marion turned and glared at Jennie and Beth.

Good. Get mad at them for a change.

Jennie's mother folded her arms. It was a sign of trouble.

Here it comes. Sam groaned. *Lecture number 942.*

Mrs. Levinsky started tapping her foot. Another bad sign. "Just what were you two girls doing out of bed?"

I'm not listening to any lectures. Sam closed her eyes. *Tell her about the lake monsters, Jennie.*

Jennie took a deep breath. "Remember the old diary we found?"

Her parents nodded.

"Well ... Ruth said she was scared of the evil in the lake." Jennie looked at Beth for help.

"And we thought we found out what the evil was," added Beth in a small voice.

Sam nudged Jennie's knee. *Get to the cave part.*

Jennie blushed. "W-we found a cave along the river and we saw a glow m-moving under the water."

"That was us!" exclaimed Bill. "We were using underwater lights!"

Oh, sure. Like we believe that.

Jennie blushed.

Beth chewed her thumbnail. "Then it was you we saw come up out of the water," she said slowly.

"Of course it was us!" snapped Marion. "Who did you think it was?"

"W-we thought you were a lake monster," stammered Jennie.

Noel and Jason hooted. Sam shot them a terrible look.

"Ruth's diary said an old prospector was scared of something evil in this lake," added Beth. "He painted a huge face on a rock to ward off the evil spirits."

Suddenly Jennie's parents were interested. They asked all kinds of questions about the diary and the cave and the prospector. Jennie and Beth told them everything.

"I'm going to ask Mrs. Anderson if we can keep that diary for a while," said Jennie's mother. "It's fascinating!"

"Did you see the kids in the cave?" Mr. Levinsky asked the divers.

Bill and Marion nodded. "Of course. But we don't pay any attention to rowboats. We just get on with our work."

"What work are you doing?" asked Mrs. Levinsky.

Who cares?

"We're studying the marine life here," explained Bill.

"And I can promise you all that there are no monsters in this lake!" added Marion, rolling her eyes.

That's what you think, lady.

Sam looked up at Jennie. *Now's the time, Jennie. Tell them about that big shadow in the water. That's proof.*

Jennie took a deep breath and told everyone about the shadow that had followed them back to the cabin.

The divers looked at each other and burst out laughing. "That's Old Harry!" Bill cried.

"He's the biggest sturgeon in the lake! People say he's almost seven feet long!" added Marion.

"I've heard about that!" cried Jennie's mom. "Every summer people try to catch that fish!"

"In fact," said Bill, "Harry is one of the reasons we're so interested in Sagawa Lake."

"Yeah," added Marion. "Conditions seem to be perfect for sturgeon here."

Bill was warming to the subject. "Did you know sturgeons can live to be more than a hundred and fifty years old?"

"I didn't know that!" exclaimed Jennie's dad.

Sam groaned. *Now they're going to talk about some fat old fish. Ask me if I care.*

Sam tuned everybody out. *Blah. Blah. Blah. I know a monster when I see one.*

I hate grown-ups.

They're such know-it-alls.

22. Henry's Last Words

The next morning they loaded Henry's motorboat and got ready to leave.

Every time their parents were out of earshot, Noel snickered about monsters. "I see one behind that tree!" he guffawed.

"Very funny, Noel," muttered Jennie.

Sam sighed. *I hate teenagers more every day.*

When the motorboat was loaded, they set out across the calm water. Behind them, the motor left a bubbly trail as they moved through the silent, empty lake.

"I hate to leave," sighed Jennie's mom as she looked around. "I love it here."

Jennie's dad glanced at the rocky, pine-covered shoreline sliding past. "So do I."

Sam was grumpy. *There are monsters down there … And we're going home without a picture.*

"There are no monsters," whispered Jennie. "Forget it. Bill and Marion said we were brats."

Who cares what they think? They're going to be monster food. Then they'll believe us.

Jennie clenched her fists. "There are no monsters, Sam!" she whispered through gritted teeth.

Beth looked at the peaceful, rocky shores. "I'm not so sure, Jennie. Ruth was really scared of something evil in this lake."

She squinted down at the water. "Those divers could be wrong."

They are wrong. And they're going to end up as somebody's dinner.

Sam sniffed to herself. *Serves them right. I've never met anybody so snooty.*

Just then the motor slowed. Jennie, Beth and Sam looked up to see that they were back at Henry's dock. On the hill, the van was parked where they had left it.

"Henry!" Mr. Levinsky called.

Like the last time, Henry came out of the cabin and spat into the weeds beside the door. He squinted at them. "Going home, are you?"

Mr. and Mrs. Levinsky nodded and asked everyone to help unload the boat.

Henry limped down to the dock and grinned oddly at Jennie and Beth.

So, what's up with this guy?

Then Henry narrowed his eyes at the girls. "Well, kids ... Did something chase you away?"

Noel and Jason chuckled as they hoisted bags onto their shoulders. "Yeah," chortled Noel. "These dopes thought they found a lake monster!"

Henry's bushy eyebrows shot up. "Maybe they did," he said mysteriously.

Speechless, Noel and Jason just looked at each other. Then they both shrugged and started up the hill to the van.

Henry watched them go before he turned back to the girls. "See any shadows alongside your boat by any chance?"

The girls gasped.

Sam stiffened. *I knew it!*

"We know what that was, Henry," laughed Mrs. Levinsky. "That's Old Harry, the huge sturgeon. You can't fool us."

Henry turned his watery eyes to Jennie's mom. "Maybe it was Harry and maybe it wasn't." He chewed his tobacco slowly.

Sam nudged Jennie. *See! This guy knows there are monsters! Even if you don't!*

Jennie grabbed Sam's collar and pulled. "It's just some stupid big fish that nobody can catch!" she hissed in Sam's ear.

"You can't scare us with those tourist stories, Henry," chuckled Jennie's dad heartily as he lifted bags. "Time to go, everybody. We have a long drive ahead of us. Thanks for renting us the boat, Henry!"

Wait a minute! Sam tried to dig her toenails

into the boards of the dock as Jennie pulled.

"Push her, Beth," grunted Jennie. "There are no monsters and I'm not letting Noel laugh at me anymore."

Beth pushed.

I really should bite these two.

Henry winked at the girls and shook his wild head. "Remember, the lake has secrets," he grinned.

"We'll remember," laughed Mrs. Levinsky.

Henry didn't answer. He chuckled loudly to himself as he limped back to the shanty. "I'm glad you kids didn't try to swim!" he called back over his shoulder.

The cabin door closed, but Henry's chuckling could still be heard through the open windows.

Sam whammed into Jennie's leg. *See! Henry knows there's a bunch of monsters in this lake!*

"Quiet, Sam!" hissed Jennie. "Don't ever mention those monsters again!" Jennie shook her finger at Sam's nose. "And I mean it."

Hmph.

As Sam was pulled up the path and pushed into the van, her mind whirred with dark thoughts about her friends.

All humans are know-it-alls. Even kids.

In the van, Sam turned her back to Jennie and glared out the window at the endless forest.

I hate being a dog.

Every time I get a chance to be famous ... some human messes it up.

Spying on Dracula

Sam, Dog Detective, sniffs out adventure!

Ten-year-old Jennie Levinsky has a secret — and only her best friend, Beth, knows about it. Jennie can "hear" what her neighbor's sheepdog, Sam, is thinking! And what Sam is thinking leads the girls into an exciting adventure at the spookiest house in town. Why is the house always dark? Why is a bat always hanging around? And who is that frightening creature living inside? Sam comes to the only logical conclusion — Dracula lives there!

THE GHOST OF CAPTAIN BRIGGS

Sam, Dog Detective, digs up a mystery!

Jennie and Beth are all set to enjoy their summer vacation with Sam. But how could they know that the house Jennie's family has rented was built long ago by a bloodthirsty pirate? Sam convinces Jennie that where there's a pirate, there must be buried treasure ... and a ghost guarding it. What else could explain the spooky housekeeper, the threatening notes and those eerie sounds coming from the attic? Then Sam digs up a hidden tunnel ... but does it lead to treasure or danger?

STRANGE NEIGHBORS

Sam is spellbound by another mystery!

There's a mystery brewing right next door to Sam the sheepdog! Three very odd women have moved in with all sorts of caged animals. Sam is sure her creepy new neighbors are witches. After all, those poor animals look so miserable they must be under a spell. Suddenly Sam isn't feeling well either. Have the witches put a hex on her, too? Can Sam, together with Jennie and her best friend, Beth, discover the truth before it's too late?

ALIENS IN WOODFORD

Sam spots another mystery and lands in the dog house!

There are strange goings-on at Woodford's abandoned airfield — unexplained lights, transport trucks rumbling about in the middle of the night and security guards who seem to have superhuman strength. For Sam, the sheepdog, it can mean only one thing — an alien invasion is on the way. In fact, the aliens may have already beamed up a couple of neighborhood pets!

Is Sam going to be the next to disappear? Can Jennie and Beth save Sam from a fate worse than dog food?

A Weekend at the Grand Hotel

Sam spies a whole heap of trouble!

What could be more exciting than the bustling lobby of the Grand Hotel? Guests arrive, people meet — and signals are exchanged. For Sam, Dog Detective, this can mean only one thing: spies, and lots of them! Why else would people be passing envelopes back and forth, sneaking into guests' rooms and using the back stairs instead of the elevator? Something's definitely up, and Sam is sure to figure it out — if only Jennie and Beth will help her.